REX E. DOODLE'S NEW BEST FRIEND

REX E. DOODLE'S NEW BEST FRIEND

Story by

JoAnn Roselli

Illustrated by

Johnny Fazzingo

REAL LIFE PETS
CHILDREN'S
BOOKS

Real Life Pets Rex & Curly

Rex E. Doodle and his friend Curly are real life lizard friends. Every day, they spend time together and enjoy the sunny garden. Sometimes, Curly, the wild lizard enters Rex's cage and sits with him on the log. Their friendship inspired this story. We hope you enjoy it! You can see more pictures of them and our other Real Life Pets at https://reallifepetsbooks.com.

Once upon a time, there was a bearded dragon named Rex who was kept in a cage outside its home.

Everyday, the bearded dragon would be given delicious-food and pet by its human parents with kindness and love.

One day, a wild curly-tailed lizard unexpectedly appeared in the garden where the Bearded Dragon lived.

The little creature had been curious about the caged one, so he decided to approach it carefully since it was big, spiky, and a little scary looking.

The bearded dragon was much larger than any of the other yard lizards and had a big triangle-shaped head and spikes along the sides of his face and all the way down his body to his thick tail.

Rex noticed the cute little lizard looking at him, so he decided to say hello.

"Hi, I'm Rex. Who are you? What's your name?"

The curly tailed lizard blushed and said, "I don't know. I never had a name."

"I'm going to call you Curly because of your curly tail," Rex said.

"Ok, I like that!" Curly giggled. Soon enough, Rex and Curly got comfortable talking and sharing stories of their different lives.

Curly was amazed by the life that the bearded dragon had - not just because of the delicious food he was served every day or his safe, cozy home, but mostly because of all the love and affection his human parents gave him every day.

On the other hand, the Bearded dragon admired how free the wild lizard was; he envied how he could freely explore without being worried of any danger or boundaries.

"Your humans must really love you," Curly said softly. "I wish I had humans to feed me and pet me and protect me like that."

"Yeah, it's nice," said Rex. "But sometimes I really wish I could be free to go anywhere and do anything, like you."

"Freedom is great, but love is better. Nobody loves me," said Curly sadly.

"I love you, Curly. You're my best friend!" Rex told him with a smile.

Because Curly was so small he was able to walk right between the bars of Rex's cage and sat on the log next to the big, spiky dragon. Curly was so happy, he wanted to get closer to his new best friend.

"I would give you a hug, but I can't because of all your spikes! I'm afraid I'd hurt myself!" Curly told Rex with a giggle.

"My mom says I have spikes because I'm so soft and squishy I'd have no other way to protect myself. I look scary so other animals won't dare to mess with me. You don't have any spikes. How do you protect yourself?" Rex asked Curly.

"Well, I don't have spikes but I can let my tail fall off to distract an animal that's trying to catch me. If they grab my tail, I can make it fall right off and run away.

Of course, I can only do that once because my tail won't grow back!"

"If you lost your tail, then I guess I couldn't call you Curly anymore!" Rex laughed.

Curly laughed even harder and said, "You could still call me Curly. I like that name."

The two became friends quickly as they realized they each had something unique to share in their conversations. Curly giggled uncontrollably when he overheard Rex's mom when she came out to serve his morning breakfast.

"Good morning, my little Rexydoodle! Oh, you have a new friend! How cute!" She put a bowl of crunchy worms in the cage and tickled Rex's stubbly chin with her finger.

Rex looked up at her with love and a tinge of embarrassment.

As Rex's mom locked the cage and walked back toward the house, Curly laughed again and asked, "What's a Rexydoodle?"

Rex replied sheepishly, "It's just her little nickname for me. Kind of silly, I know. But she means well."

The next day Curly returned to visit his new friend. It was a beautiful, sunny day and the two lizard buddies enjoyed basking in the warm sunshine together.

But soon enough - things were about to change when a Great Snowy Egret appeared low in the sky above them, searching for food in the garden area.

Scared and unsure of what to do, poor little Curly sat still, wondering if the great bird had seen him.

Knowing his buddy was in trouble, Rex shouted, "Curly! Run!"

Scared and confused, little Curly took off running in the wrong direction! Instead of heading toward the safety of Rex's cage, he ran out into the garden.

The hungry egret was fast behind him, swooping down and almost catching the little curly-tailed lizard in his long, pointy beak!

The hungry egret swooped down and chased Curly, trying to catch his tail with its long, orange beak!

Curly ran as fast as he could, but the long-legged egret was catching up.

Just when it seemed he would surely be caught, his best friend had a brilliant idea.

Quick-thinking Rex knew there was only one way for his little buddy to get out of this scary situation.

"Drop your tail, Curly!" he shouted to his friend.

Curly yanked off his squiggly little tail and threw it into the air to distract the hungry egret. Wiggling and squiggling like an airborne earthworm, the tail was just the thing to distract the egret so Curly could try to get back to the safety of Rex's cage.

The confused egret saw the curly tail flying through the air over his head...

so it jumped up into the air and grabbed the squiggly, wiggly tail and flew off happily with his catch-of-the-day.

Now that the egret was busy catching Curly's tail, he had just enough time to run to Rex's cage and squeeze between the bars to safety.

Happy with his catch, the great white egret flew off into the bright blue sky.

Curly was so tired from his scary experience that he had to lie down on the floor of the cage to catch his breath.

Rex was very worried about his little buddy, but so glad that he was going to be okay!

Although Curly and Rex thought the big, scary egret was having Curly's tail for lunch, the truth was that she was actually a caring mama bird who brought her catch back to the nest to feed her hungry baby egrets.

"Whew! That was close!" Curly exclaimed, relieved to be safe by his best friend's spikey side.

"You did it, Curly! Wow! Does it hurt?" Rex asked.

"I don't feel any different. A little lighter, maybe." Curly looked back to see his curly little tail was no longer there.

The two friends sat together in the safety of the cage, when Curly noticed a sign that said "No Regrets".

"I have an idea!," he said. "I'll be right back."

Clever Curly crossed out the "R" so the sign now read, "No Egrets!" That ought to keep them away, he thought.

Back in the cage, the lizards talked about how even though they had different lifestyles, they had more in common than they'd thought. Just then, an odd looking bird came waddling up to the cage.

"Hey Curly," Rex said, "I think we're going to need another sign!" The friends giggled from the safety of the cage they now shared, while the goofy duck quacked and walked away.